D1440530

Raintree is an imprint of Capstone Global Library Limited, a company
incorporated in England and Wales having its registered office at 7
Pilgrim Street, London, EC4V 6LB - Registered company number: 6695582

www.raintree.co.uk
myorders@raintree.co.uk

Text © Capstone Global Library Limited 2016
The moral rights of the proprietor have been asserted.

All rights reserved. No part of this publication may be reproduced in any
form or by any means (including photocopying or storing it in any medium
by electronic means and whether or not transiently or incidentally to
some other use of this publication) without the written permission of
the copyright owner, except in accordance with the provisions of the
Copyright, Designs and Patents Act 1988 or under the terms of a licence
issued by the Copyright Licensing Agency, Saffron House, 6-10 Kirby
Street, London EC1N 8TS (www.cla.co.uk). Applications for the copyright
owner's written permission should be addressed to the publisher.

Designed by Hilary Wacholz
Original illustrations © Capstone 2016
Illustrated by Kirbi Fagan
Design Elements: Shutterstock: In·Finity, zelimirz, vladis.studio,
NEGOVURA, IhorZigor, astudio, Thomas Bethge

ISBN 978 1 4747 1046 6 (paperback)
19 18 17 16 15
10 9 8 7 6 5 4 3 2 1

British Library Cataloguing in Publication Data
A full catalogue record for this book is available from
the British Library.

Printed and bound in China.

VOLCANO
A FIERY TALE OF SURVIVAL

> BY THOMAS KINGSLEY TROUPE

> ILLUSTRATED BY KIRBI FAGAN

SURVIVE!

raintree
a Capstone company — publishers for children

CONTENTS

CHAPTER 1

INACTIVE

"So it's not even an active volcano?" Cam Peterson asked.

Cam's mum laughed and lowered the sun visor in the car. "No," she said. "But we probably wouldn't be visiting somewhere that had an active volcano. I doubt we'd want to return a melted hire car to the airport."

Cam's dad pulled the car into the small car park and turned the engine off. It was bright and beautiful on the island, just like it had been every day so far. Cam was amazed by how far he could see, even from his back seat window.

He wasn't excited about the stop they had decided to make. After all, every little "adventure" they went on during their holiday was less time spent on the beach. Cam wasn't sure how long it would be until they'd get to go to the sea again, so wasting time to see something that sort of looked like a volcano wasn't his idea of a good time.

"All right," Dad said, opening his door. "Let's take a look."

Cam climbed out of the car and walked to the edge of the empty car park. It didn't seem like anyone else was interested in Mount Palahara, either. His dad had a knack for finding sites that weren't exactly popular.

He looked up to see his parents walking over to a big wooden sign. On it was a faded map of Mount Palahara. As he got closer, Cam was able to see more detail.

"Palahara is a shield volcano," his mum read, tracing the words with her finger. She murmured through the parts she didn't think were interesting. "It hasn't erupted for over five hundred years."

Cam half-listened, hoping he'd be able to look into the mouth of the volcano, at least. He was fairly certain he wouldn't see anything cool like lava, but he thought it was probably worth a peek. As his parents marvelled at the altitude and the road they'd taken to get there, Cam walked up the worn steps to the observation platform.

A number of small signs suggested that he was heading towards a fantastic photo opportunity. *We'll see about that,* he thought.

Cam got to the octagon-shaped cement slab at the top of the steps. He was disappointed to see that it was fenced off with a safety rail on all sides.

Cam smirked. *Wouldn't want anyone to fall into the inactive volcano!* he thought, leaning over the rail. He looked down and was surprised to see plant life at the basin.

No hot lava. No spouting geyser of destruction. Just pretty plants.

"Sigh," Cam mumbled. For the first time, he realized how out of breath he was.

It wasn't like he'd run up all the steps, but just being at such a high elevation really gave his lungs a workout.

His parents had finally made their way up to the platform. "So, what do you think, Cam?" Dad said. "Pretty cool, huh?"

"Yep," Cam said, trying to sound enthused. "It's pretty cool."

"Your mum thought you'd think it was boring," Dad said, pointing his thumb in mum's direction.

Cam squinted in the bright afternoon sun. "Well, it's my first volcano," he said. "So there's that."

The three of them stood alone at the top of Mount Palahara, looking down at the rest of the island. After a few minutes of searching, they were able to find their hotel along the ocean's coastline.

Okay then, Cam thought. *Let's get back there.*

CHAPTER 2

SANDCASTLES

At Cam's insistence, the Petersons spent the rest of the afternoon relaxing on the beach. Cam hit the waves with a body board, played some beach volleyball with a few older kids, and snorkelled until he couldn't swim another stroke.

Cam's parents sat on their sun loungers under the parasol. Cam was collapsed near a sandcastle he'd got tired of building about halfway through.

"Are you going to finish that thing?" came a voice from his left. Cam was so exhausted he almost couldn't open his eyes.

"I'm not eating anything," Cam said. He was used to his dad asking him to finish his food at restaurants.

"The sandcastle," the voice said. In a daze, Cam realized it was a girl's voice. When he opened his eyes, he saw a ten-year-old girl was standing near his half-finished castle. Her hair was wet, her knees were sandy and she carried a small plastic bucket. The plastic spade was visible in the bucket.

"Oh," Cam said. "No. I've finished. Go ahead."

The girl nodded. Without another word, she set to work. Cam sat up and watched her. She patted the sides of the wall down to smooth the surface. At one point she got up and filled her bucket with sea water. He couldn't work out why until he saw her carve out an elaborate moat around the entire structure.

"Are you sure you don't want to help?" the girl asked. "It is your castle, after all."

"Nope," Cam said. "It's definitely your castle now. You're good at this. What's your name?"

The girl looked up from her work. She wiped a wet strand of hair from her eyes.

"I'm Amy," she said. "We're from Pittsburgh."

"Hi, Amy," he said. "I'm Cam from Topeka."

"Kansas," Amy said. "They made us memorize all the states and capitals of the USA last year."

"Nice," Cam said. "I can't remember the capital of Pittsburgh."

Amy stared at him for a moment. "Pittsburgh's not a –"

"I know it's a city in Pennsylvania," Cam said. "Just seeing if you were paying attention."

"Funny," Amy said. She went back to work.

As Cam watched Amy add more parts to the castle, he felt the sand beneath him begin to rumble, as if something big and ugly was living under the surface. A moment later, it was still again.

"Whoa," Cam said. "Did you feel that?"

Amy nodded. "Probably a small earthquake," she said. "The island does that sometimes."

Cam looked around. No one else on the beach seemed bothered by it.

Where Cam was from, the worst thing they had to worry about were tornadoes. Those came down from the skies, not up from the ground.

It was the first time Cam felt like the ground he walked upon wasn't exactly stable. It was unnerving to say the least.

CHAPTER 3

FIRE FEAST

By the time it started to get dark on the island, Cam had all but forgotten about Amy and her amazing sandcastle skills. His parents were changing from their tacky-looking island T-shirts into different tacky-looking island T-shirts.

"Are you sure you don't want to go with us?" Dad asked. "It's going to be pretty cool."

Cam was lying face down on his bed on a pillow in the hotel room. He was so exhausted from a full day at the beach and the high-altitude volcano trip that he didn't know if he could ever get up again.

"No," Cam said, his voice muffled by his pillow. "I don't even want to move."

"But it's the Fire Feast," Mum said. "They say it's one of those things that tourists shouldn't miss."

Cam rolled over onto his back and groaned. In addition to being worn out, he had more than a little bit of a sunburn on his back.

"I think I'll be okay," Cam mumbled. "You two should go."

"Cam," Dad said, frowning. "They juggle fire and dance around and stuff. I've seen videos online. It's crazy."

"I'll check a look online," Cam said. "I'm tired."

His mum sat down on the edge of the bed and opened up a flashy leaflet for the Fire Feast. It showed a group of people dressed in traditional island wear. One of them was shooting fire out of his mouth.

"Wow," Cam said, pointing to the fire breather. "Looks like someone had the hotel's spicy tacos!"

Cam's dad winced, clutching his stomach. "We don't need to mention those ever again."

"They're going to have all kinds of different food there," Mum said. It seemed she didn't want to talk about the tacos anymore, either. "Look."

Cam sat up to look at the leaflet. There were loads of foods he couldn't even begin to name. The crowning jewel of the leaflet was the roasted pig clutching an apple in its mouth. Cam wondered if they'd bribed the pig with the piece of fruit before sending it to the flames.

"Definitely going to sit this one out," Cam said. "I'll get some food from the vending machine downstairs. Okay?"

He watched as his parents looked at each other and communicated between themselves without saying a word. Finally, after a shrug from his dad, his mum spoke.

"Fine," she said. "But I don't want you playing video games all night. Mix it up a bit, perhaps? Read a book for an hour, maybe?"

"We're on holiday, Mum," Cam said. She gave him the disapproving Mum look, and he gave in. "Okay, okay. I'll read a little, too."

To prove he was a man of his word, Cam opened up his book and jumped back into reading. It was about a child who woke up with superpowers and was suddenly expected to protect the entire world.

When his parents had finished getting ready, Cam's mum left him some money on the side table. "That's for dinner," she said. "Not for the video games downstairs."

"Or for sweets," Dad added. "Eat a sandwich or something first, at least."

"I'll remember to sit up straight, too," Cam said sarcastically. Then, in a more sincere tone, added, "Have fun, you two."

"You too," Mum said. She kissed Cam on his forehead.

Cam gasped. "Ow, Mum!" he said, playing up the pain. "My sunburn."

"Stay out of trouble," Dad said, not convinced. "We'll be back in a few hours."

And just like that, Cam was on his own. He breathed a long sigh of relief.

CHAPTER 4

EXPLOSION!

Half an hour later, Cam was almost at the end of the third chapter. He had ended up rereading the same paragraph nearly twelve times before he realized that the book wasn't going to keep him awake. Throwing in the towel, he set the book aside and rested his eyes for a moment.

As soon as he began to drift off to sleep, he felt the entire hotel shake. Cam's eyes snapped open and he sat up, looking around. The room was still, but he was wide awake.

Did I just dream that? Cam wondered.

Nothing in the room seemed out of place, and he couldn't hear sirens or anything that he assumed would announce the arrival of an earthquake. He wasn't sure. In Kansas, when someone spotted a tornado, weather sirens would ring out one after another.

"Maybe they only do that for tornadoes," he said to himself.

Cam got up off the bed with a groan. His shorts were still a little damp from the sea, but he was too tired and sunburned to do anything about it.

He walked over to the sliding glass door and pulled it open. He took a few steps onto the small deck ten floors above the hotel's island-themed property.

Below him, he could see people swimming in the illuminated pool. The thatch huts they used to serve drinks and snacks were lit up with multi-coloured bulbs. Cam looked over to the left. The Fire Feast was already underway. Just as his dad had said, there were people playing with fire on the stage.

"Cool," Cam said, feeling as though he was the only one missing out. Even the poor roasted pig was in attendance.

As he slid the door shut, an explosion shook the entire hotel. It felt as though a superhero had power-punched the side of the building.

Cam jumped back as the glass on the patio door shattered. Shards fell into the room, so he quickly pulled on his sandals.

Cam looked around, uncertain what had happened or what he should do. It sounded like the people in the rooms next to his were scurrying around. Afraid to peek his head out through the jagged opening in the patio door, he stood back a metre or so and tried to look outside.

Amazingly, the island seemed to be glowing a little brighter. It was like the flames from the Fire Feast were lighting up the rest of the island. The sky had gone from purple to a dark shade of orange.

Down at the Fire Feast, people were gathered around and looking up at something he couldn't see.

But even from ten floors up, Cam could tell they were pointing at the sky.

Maybe a plane crash? Cam wondered. That would explain the explosion. He remembered that the airport was quite close to the island's mountains.

Cam went to the hotel room door. He peeked out through the peephole. He could see people running past the door, moving quickly. He put his hand on the door handle to open it for a better look.

A second explosion rocked the hotel, almost knocking Cam to the ground.

Definitely not a plane, Cam realized.

CHAPTER 5

HOT RESCUE

Cam got to his feet and opened the door. An older man and woman ran past, heading for the hotel's lift. He watched as they continually pushed the DOWN button.

That, more than anything, made Cam freak out.

"What's going on?" Cam shouted to the couple.

The older lady didn't say anything. Her eyes remained on the display above the lift's doors.

"Hey, can you hear me?" Cam shouted louder.

"The volcano has erupted!" the old man shouted. "The whole side of the mountain has blown open."

Cam thought the man must be crazy. He knew they had to be talking about Mount Palahara as it was the closest and biggest volcano, but that couldn't be right. Palahara was a shield volcano – and a dormant one, at that.

And we were just there, Cam thought. *It looked pretty inactive to me.*

Before he could say another word, the lift door opened and the couple wedged their way in. As the doors closed, Cam remained standing in the doorway of his room.

"So where are they going?" Cam said to himself.

Cam didn't know much about volcanoes, but he knew he didn't want to be outside when one erupted.

A door across the corridor from his room opened. A familiar face peeked out. "Amy?" Cam said. "What's going on?"

Amy braced herself against the doorway as another explosion rocked the building. Alarms rang out in the corridors and he heard more glass shatter throughout their floor.

As Cam stepped out of his room, he heard something big hammer into the side of the building. Amy's door shut. Cam heard her scream from the other side.

"Hey!" Cam shouted, running to her door. "Open up! Are you okay?"

Cam tried the door, but it was locked. He jiggled the handle and beat the side of his fist against the keycard reader. Nothing happened. Before long, the corridor began to fill with smoke.

Is there a fire? Cam wondered.

"Amy!" Cam said, realizing his own hotel room door had closed shut, locking him out. "Open the door. We have to get out of here!"

Cam couldn't hear anything else over the wails of the sirens and the shouts of people running past.

Cam tried the door again, but it wouldn't budge. Amy wasn't safe in there – he had to find a way to help her.

The hotel shook again, throwing Cam against the wall. The lights above blinked a few times, and then went out completely. A few seconds later, dimmer lights lit the corridor.

I have to get her out, Cam thought. He raised his foot to kick in the door.

THUD! As his foot made contact with the door, he fell. He stood up to try again – but the door popped open.

"Cam?" Amy asked. "What are we going to do?"

Before she could say another word or close the door on him again, Cam pushed his way into her hotel room. He couldn't see her parents, and wondered if they were at the Fire Feast like his were.

Cam was about to grab her hand and pull her away when he saw something unbelievable through the window in Amy's room.

It looked like the end of the world.

The sky seemed to be on fire, glowing orange from the wound on the side of Mount Palahara.

Steaming, molten lava poured from the volcano's wound, leaving bright trails like tendrils down the massive hill.

All the trees caught in the flow's path were burning like torches along the slopes.

Buildings that Cam didn't recognize were on fire, and chunks of glowing rock streamed in all directions through the air.

That old man was right, Cam thought.

CHAPTER 6

VOLCANIC COMETS

"Everything is burning!" Amy cried, stumbling towards the patio door.

Cam couldn't argue with her. It didn't look exactly safe outside the hotel, so he thought the best thing to do was to stay put and wait until things calmed down.

"I hope my parents are okay," Cam whispered.

"Mine are at that flaming food thing," Amy said quietly.

"The Fire Feast," Cam said.

"Whatever it's called," Amy said. "Now *everything* is on fire."

The building lurched as if it were on stilts. He had no idea if that was another earthquake, or what. As he considered what to do, another explosion rocked the hotel – one that made the others before it seem like gentle taps.

Glass all around them shattered. Pieces of the ceiling came down in chunky, dusty showers. Massive rocks shot out from the volcano at impossible angles across the island city. Flaming trails followed, making them look like confused comets. It was like a meteor shower was happening right before their eyes.

Cam's eyes went wide. "They're heading towards the hotel," he said. "We have to –"

Cam was interrupted by a fiery chunk of rock slamming into the side of the hotel. Out of sight, other projectiles made contact as well. The force of the volcanic attack knocked him and Amy to the carpet.

Cam sat up, completely stunned. The wall where the window gave them a view of the volcano was obliterated, along with the ceiling above it and the floor below. Flames licked at the raw opening and smoke poured through it. With the side of the hotel blown open, Cam heard rescue vehicles wailing in the distance. People outside were shouting.

"This cannot be happening," he whispered.

The ground beneath their feet shifted. "I think the hotel is falling apart," Amy whispered, picking herself up. She coughed, covering her mouth from the smoke and dust.

"You're right," Cam said. He drew his arm across his mouth and looked around for the bathroom door. He darted towards it, careful to avoid the small pools of flame forming near the destroyed wall.

"Where are you going?" Amy shouted. "We have to get out of here!"

"I know!" Cam shouted. He looked around the dark bathroom frantically until his bare toes touched towels on the floor.

With quick hands, Cam snapped up the towels and turned the bathroom taps on. Luckily, the water was still on. He stuck the towels under the water, soaking them as best he could.

The ground shifted again and the smoke grew thicker. The air started to sting his eyes.

Before Amy could say anything else, he left the bathroom and threw a towel to her.

"Here," he said, wrapping his towel around his head, covering his mouth. "Do what I'm doing. We're going to get out of here."

By the time Amy had her head-wrap secured, Cam noticed that his trick was working. It was easier to breathe in the horrible air with something wet in front of his mouth.

With Amy ready, Cam opened the door and led her into the tenth-floor corridor.

CHAPTER 7

COMING DOWN

Cam and Amy raced down the corridor, zigzagging around the debris that had fallen from the ceiling. They leapt over a fallen plant before reaching the hotel's lifts.

Amy pushed the *DOWN* button and looked up at the display. None of the floor numbers were lit up. She pushed it again as if that would turn the lift back on.

"I don't think it's working," Cam said gently to Amy.

Looking around, Cam spotted a door a metre or so further down the corridor. The sign showed a stick figure heading down some steps. Above the sign were the words *IN CASE OF FIRE, USE STAIRS.*

Does a volcano eruption count as a fire? Cam wondered, only half-joking.

Cam shoved the door open, helped Amy through the opening, and followed closely behind. As the door slammed behind them, he wondered if they were ever going to make it to the ground floor before the building collapsed.

"C'mon," Amy shouted. "We have to find my parents!"

"Mine too," Cam cried.

As Cam's feet hit the first landing, he wished he'd worn something other than sandals. As he descended the second set of steps, he thought about all of the stuff he'd left back in his room. Considering the pelting the hotel had taken, he had his doubts that there'd be anything left.

The hotel shook again. Columns of dust streamed down from the steps above them. A horrifying thought struck Cam: *What if the steps cracked and fell on top of us?*

"Faster!" Cam shouted, trying not to think about anything at all.

"I'm going as fast as I can!" Amy cried. She was holding the handrails with one hand while struggling to keep her wet towel wrap over her face with the other.

Cam squinted in the low emergency light. He heard people on the steps above and below them. Everyone was looking to escape, but what would they do once they got outside?

He knew that lava was slow moving. Even so, with the air full of smoke and toxic fumes, he wasn't sure being outside would be much better.

On the way down, Cam and Amy helped a few people to their feet. One woman was coughing so badly that he stopped, tore his wet towel in two, and gave her a half.

After what seemed like forever, they finally reached the bottom floor.

"It says emergency exit," Amy said, pausing. "Alarm will sound."

Cam caught himself hesitating at first too. Then he shook his head, took a deep breath, and shoved the bar to open the door. A small, shrill alarm bleated for a moment or two before silencing itself.

The door opened onto a pavement along the side of the hotel. As they stepped out into the glowing night, Cam's jaw dropped.

"No way," he said.

CHAPTER 8

LAVA TOWN

It was one thing seeing the damage and the chaos from ten floors up. Now, on ground level and outside, Cam was in the thick of it.

"This is insane," Cam whispered.

Everywhere was in upheaval. A fire crew was battling the flames of a restaurant Cam's family had eaten at the day before. People were running down the street, shouting the names of people they were looking for. A car lay near by, completely crushed by a still-glowing mass of rock.

In the distance, but hovering above the town like a wounded giant, was Mount Palahara. A giant chasm gaped open in the side of the volcano, spewing out a steady stream of glowing lava. Black smoke billowed from the edges.

"It's snowing," Amy whispered, pointing at the sky. "It's not supposed to snow here."

Cam watched a few flakes drop onto his shoulders. When he touched it, he realized what it actually was.

Looking around, Cam saw that there was a layer of ash covering everything. "Ash," he said. "Not snow."

Something big and heavy landed with a *THUNK!* a metre to his right. He looked up and saw huge chunks of the hotel falling from above.

"C'mon!" Cam cried. "Let's head towards the water!"

The two of them raced through the ashen chaos, squeezing past others.

Everyone in sight seemed desperate to be somewhere else – anywhere but where they were.

When they reached the back of the hotel, they saw steam rising rapidly from the pool. People in swimming suits watched the hotel and the sky nervously, as if unable to decide whether they should stay near the pool or go elsewhere for cover.

"Dad!" Cam shouted, immediately realizing how pointless it was. There were probably hundreds of people within earshot who were dads. It wasn't going to be that easy to find his parents – or Amy's.

The ground rumbled again. People shouted and screamed. As Cam looked up, he watched a gigantic chunk of the hotel come falling to the ground. A moment later, the chunk of debris slammed into the concrete patio behind the building.

Cam didn't want to think about whether there were people still standing where the hunk of hotel had fallen. He just kept his eyes open, looking around for –

"Cam!" came a voice.

Cam turned to look. He blinked hard, unable to trust his eyes. When Cam opened them again, he saw his parents running towards him through the crowd.

They both had flowered garlands around their necks, but neither of them looked like themselves. Their faces and hair were covered in ash, and their colourful T-shirts were sooty and drab now.

Cam ran to his parents. They both checked him over with their hands, making sure he wasn't hurt. "This is Amy," Cam said. Amy nodded shyly.

Cam's dad placed a hand on her head. "They're trying to keep everyone by the sea," he said to them, unable to take his eyes off of the volcano. "People were trying to break through the barricades to get to the hotel while screaming that their loved ones were inside."

"That's a death sentence," Cam said. "It felt like the hotel was going to –"

A loud cracking sound made all of them turn their heads.

Cam, Amy, and Cam's parents watched in horror as the top three floors of the hotel collapsed on top of each other.

Amy gasped. "What if my mum and dad went after me?" she cried.

"I'm sure they're at the beach, waiting," Cam said. "We should go there right now to look for them."

Amy nodded, tears cutting clean paths down her ashen face.

★ ★ ★

Hours after Mount Palahara had calmed down, the city continued to burn. Meanwhile, the Anderson family searched through the crowd, looking for Joe and Regina Madden, Amy's parents.

After they'd combed nearly all the navigable terrain in sight, they were about to give up their search. Cam had no idea what he was going to say to Amy. Of course, it was possible her parents were still alive, but the odds seemed slim at best.

Just then, Amy spotted a couple hunched over on the beach, watching the sea. Their bodies were shaking with sobs.

"That's them," Amy whispered. Then she cried out, "Mum! Dad!"

At the sound of Amy's voice, the two hunched over adults looked up and turned around. Both of them scrambled to their feet, slipping in the sand, and ran to their daughter. Cam watched as they lifted Amy up and wrapped her tightly in their arms.

"When we saw the upper floors," Amy's mum said shakily, "we..."

Her dad slowly shook his head. "We assumed the worst," he finished, placing an arm around his wife's shoulders.

Amy introduced her parents to Cam and his family. Twice, Amy told them that Cam was the hero who'd gotten her out of the hotel safely.

Regina and Joe Madden thanked Cam profusely, hugging him as if he were family.

"I owed her one," Cam said, relief and exhaustion mingling in his heart.

Amy grinned.

VOLCANO SURVIVAL

It's hard to imagine anything more terrifying than getting caught near an erupting volcano. However, there are things you can do – and carry with you – to increase your chances of survival.

Awareness: Of course, the best way to avoid a volcanic eruption is to stay away from active volcanoes! But if that's not possible, then it's important to know where any active, nearby volcanoes are located.

Warning systems: If you do live near a volcano, find out what kind of alarm your community uses in case of an eruption. Most use sirens, but regions vary, so it's important to know what to listen or watch out for.

Evacuation: With your family, draw up a household evacuation plan – and make sure you familiarize yourself with the evacuation procedure for your area.

First aid kit: The kit should include batteries, a radio and any necessary medications. Bottled water and non-perishable food should also be stored near by.

Clothing: It goes without saying that lava or magma should be given a wide berth, but having a pair of sturdy boots and a pair of goggles on hand is wise. Most importantly, given the amount of ash that will be in the air, make sure you have a respirator for each family member.

Shelter: If emergency services indicate you should not evacuate, stay inside! If you do end up getting caught outside during an eruption, seek high ground as far away from the eruption site as is possible.

ABOUT THE AUTHOR

Thomas Kingsley Troupe has written more than thirty children's books. His book *Legend of the Werewolf* (Picture Window Books, 2011) received a bronze medal for the Moonbeam Children's Book Award. Thomas lives in Minnesota, USA, with his wife and two sons.

ABOUT THE ILLUSTRATOR

Kirbi Fagan is a vintage-inspired artist living in the Detroit, Michigan area of the USA. She is an award-winning illustrator who specializes in creating art for young readers. Her work is known for magical themes, vintage textures, bright colours and powerful characterization. She received her bachelor's degree in Illustration from Kendall College of Art and Design, USA. Kirbi lives by two words: "Spread joy". She is known to say, "I'm in it with my whole heart". When not illustrating, Kirbi enjoys writing stories, spending time with her family and rollerblading with her dog, Sophie.

GLOSSARY

altitude height of something relative to sea level

debris pieces that are left after something has been destroyed

eruption sending out of ash, rocks and lava from a volcano

geyser hole in the ground that shoots out hot water and steam

lava melted rock from a volcano

obliterated completely destroyed

projectile something that is shot outwards with explosive speed

unnerving if something is unnerving to a person, it causes them to feel frightened, upset or unable to think clearly

WRITING PROMPTS

1. Pick a page from this book and rewrite it from Amy's perspective. How might she see things differently from Cam? Why?

2. When you've finished reading the volcano survival tips that immediately follow the main story, write a list of things that Cam did well and a list of things that Cam should have done differently during the eruption.

3. Write a short story about yourself where you survive a different kind of natural disaster. How do you manage to survive? You decide.

DISCUSSION QUESTIONS

1. What do you think was Cam's wisest decision in this story? What was his worst decision? Why?

2. Cam is a good person for helping Amy during the eruption. Why do you think he chose to help her?

3. Have you experienced a natural disaster? If so, talk about it. If not, what kind of natural disaster do you most hope to avoid? Why?